THE

UNIVERSE
RECREATED

SHEKHAR PAL

Woven Words Publishers OPC Pvt. Ltd.

Registered Office:

Vill: Raipur, P.O: Raipur Paschimbar,

Dist: Purba Midnapore, Pin: 721401,

West Bengal, India.

www.wovenwordspublishers.in

Email: editor@wovenwordspublishers.in

First published by Woven Words Publishers OPC Pvt. Ltd., 2018

Copyright© Shekhar Pal, 2018

NOVELLA

IMPRINT: WOVEN WORDS LAUNCHPAD

ISBN 13:978-93-86897-18-3

ISBN 10: 9386897180

Price: 10$/₹130

PROLOGUE

What about life? Isn't it being a beautiful gift that we have been enjoying for ages? We feel disturbed, we feel mingled with many harshness of life, we even sometime make ourselves quit for some time, but still we love life. Everyone loves themselves irrespective of what hardships they have gone through. Into which depth we lived our lives.

Whatever we are, we always keep dreaming. We all live in our fantasy world in which our parents also glue their hopes from us. We try to put our best in all the case. Yet we not be able to define ourselves properly. But we love our ways, we love ourselves, we love our lives.

Our dreams may be shattered but the hope to live this life remains somewhere in the form of love. Love that a mother's heart has for her children. Love that a father shows with his hard work. Love that a sister always shows with her support. Love that a boy feels for his beloved or vice-versa. Love makes us to feel this life in a better way with millions of hopes and give strength to stay strong.

15/May/2049.

2 A.M.

Hey Rudra, are you listening...? Is this mission is going to be our last one?

I mean what is a need to peep into the ass of this experiment. Everyone knows what a big bang explosion can do. I think before making this blunder, they should think twice.

Hey, are you listening Rudra, what I am talking to you? Where are you man...? Aren't you listening to me?

He blows up the horn of the military truck to wake me up from my lost world of thoughts. I was thinking of my family, about our lives, about everyone's life. About the life, what would happen if, experiment goes wrong. What, if the professor succeeds in doing the big-bang experiment, and as result of the life on the earth get destroyed I was totally lost in the fear of what would happen after the experiment.

The road was quite silent, but the sound of military filled up the whole city with the sound of horn and the distance between the laboratory and us was decreasing like the sound of the scrunches of the bundle of paper goes in our ears, while skipping its pages through the fingers. The laboratory was sealed and was announced to hand over the project safely to a big multinational corporation "FORKS". I was the head of the special team, having the most capable officers in it. All the people of that area were shifted to other cities. This has become an important issue for the whole world. Countries like America, China, Japan, Russia, having advanced technologies and having around 2000 officers, scientists, bomb diffuser were following the path to the spot with us. The night was unusual as the city has left with just the landmasses, buildings, mansions, restaurants, and nameplates of the house owners, which were of no use now. Reporters, Discoverers from all over the world were following us today.

I didn't know why, but I was just thinking about how much we would have to suffer from his success. Would all people die? Would everything decompose to hell? Well, for now, we had to be calm and focused.

'Everything will be okay, let's pray to the Almighty'. Aadi said looking at me, extending his right hand and putting it on my left shoulder.

"What is this ALMIGHTY or PRAYERES, I grinned looking out of the window. He is a latent destroyer not the almighty for me. I came out of me and opposed him bluntly, hitting my left hand on the dashboard.

He took a sharp right turn, slipping his hand from my shoulder to change the gear, accelerated the car and pushed the horn to alert the team. I could see the emptiness of the area and could feel the silence prevailing in it.

'He blesses us. He is our GOD, the one who has given us the precious life,' Aadi exclaimed.

"Bless what bless…" I looked at him sharply. Aadi, he took away my mom and dad in an accident. Why? does he has any answer for this? They were coming on my birthday to wish me when I was in college, what was my age that time? Do you remember Aadi, '17', I was just 17 then, when my roof of support and love was blown away by your so called 'Almighty'. I stopped begging for his blessings after that incident and stopped going to his place for worship. And look, I am happy, living a very successful life. I don't need the blessings of someone who took my parents away from me, making me orphan.

Yeah, I remember that day Rudra, please don't be sad for that incident. We all need you, you are the head of this mission. Aadi said looking into my eyes.

For me, from that day Aadi, the concept of 'GOD and PRAYERS' has been changed. Why God has not given an equal time span to live their life equally? They were coming to give me a surprise that day, after a whole year. I didn't even get a chance to see them alive and adieu them.

I was so much drenched in the memories of my mom and dad that I again started to narrate the same event that took years ago. But Aadi, my best friend from collage days always stood by me and offered his shoulder to rest and pour out my heart with him.

Life is so uncertain. We don't know when will the coin of our destiny topples and will show the sad part or the happy part. We need to believe in our dreams to lead the rest of our life with positive hopes.

Experiences of life are the lessons which gives the finest teachings, everyone changes with time and life experiences. There are many people suffering hardship in their life. We need to face it by a strength, 'Positivity'. I was totally broken after despair of my mom and dad.

Gloomy thoughts and somewhere this eerie experiment's thoughts were also provoking a load of anger and fear inside me. The day was full of awe. Heartbeats were faster than usual counts. the carnal strength has close to leave the hope and was like a fallen leaf of an old tree.

Finally, the professor's house came into our sight after the last left turn.

I drew my head out of the window to look at the sky that was filled with the helicopters that were patrolling over the area. Their lights have created a dramatic scene. All were tensed in that situation and were waiting for a miracle to take us over it and everyone to be safe.

I took out my wireless to contact the helicopters to lead us to the safe area. Soon the aura became hectic. I took out the loudspeaker from the car to make some announcements.

"Soldiers! Take your positions." My sound was as loud as the sound of an exhaust engine. I wanted to give all my soldiers a positive energy, with this I started a short energy provoking speech -

'Life may not be the same after this night but remember you and I will be same for tonight. The training that emanated all of us as a capable officer will be same. The vow which we have taken while joining to serve our country would be same. The humanity which we have within us would be same. Although we are going be a part of an eerie mission but believe me if we work together we can save the earth and the life. Let's follow the points we made together for this mission, let's follow the training that emanated a brave soldier and great human in us'.

'This is the spirit, Rudra', Aadi commented. When I leaned into the car to put the loud speaker back. Soon after the sound that had been coming to my ears was filled up the with the energetic sound of applauses which helped me to come out of the fear, which helped the other officers and the team to believe in each other.

The lab was more important than the professor or any other precious thing over there in the society. After covering the whole area. We entered H.No. 22-A. which was at the corner of Collins Street lane, the residence of Prof. Brij where experiment was to be tested.

He was working with a multinational company 'THE FORKS' who deal with the supply of the expensive drugs and medical instruments throughout the world.

Prof. Brij was the senior scientist and a researcher, who worked to emanate the formula to reduce the size of the tissue to a microscopic level, to make the study simpler and advance to cure the diseases that are hard to cure. His mostly experiments were usually related to save resources and to manufacture the drugs in cheap which are costly, that will also reduce the cost of treatment.

Prof. Brij had succeeded to develop a formula through his research that could reduce the size of a tissue and has also started to work on his next invention to make a tissue 'invisible'. Soon the company started to formulate such medicines and medical machinery to sell his invention to various countries to help them to come out of the problems of many incurable diseases.

After his invention, Prof. Brij was credited a lot of money and was also honored by various titles.

One day when he was working on his next invention to make a tissue invisible. 'A giant mistake occurred in the exhaust system of the lab where he was working. And the computer system had stopped working, due to which prof. Brij along with 4 other scientists who were working on the same experiment with him died due to lack of oxygen inside the lab'. This was the statement given by the company in the news and to the police after Prof. Brij and his co-worker's death.

PROF'S HOUSE

Before the secret was leaked we never thought this house could be a lab, we entered Professors house which might be a lab, everything was like a normal house. We searched every corner thoroughly, almost peeped into every small hole. The house wasn't so big and was having only ground floor and a small section above the entrance where the stairs were going.

We were tensed, so, we as a team inhaled air to calm ourselves. We were ready to check that secret place. I stepped on the first stair very silently having my training in my mind, and my gun in my right hand. I was about to put my other foot on the second ladder, I heard a soldier screaming my name. I came stepped back and followed the voice whose intensity was reducing but still making my nerves alert. For the reason of its production.

Voice was coming from professor's bedroom. There was another room inside his bedroom, a small room connected to the bedroom. The door was closed from inside. We became more sure that it must be a lab inside the small room.

Now it was the time to surrender our breaths to the danger that might be waiting for us inside the lab. The room was normal as like other rooms there. I drew my ears closer to the wooden door. I heard nothing. My mind was thinking very sharply on every small hint present over there. The bomb defusing team took their positions. They checked the door with the scanning machine. There was neither any explosive thing nor any hard thing behind the door. They broke the door, and what? We were shocked after what we saw inside the room. We entered the room, but there was no one inside it. A long wooden table having a computer with many other files on it. Along with me and Aadi five other officers entered the lab. We started searching more deeply through the files and computer. But not a single piece was there that could prove that any experiment had ever happened there. We searched the whole house again. The team was searching the lab more sharply, I came out to search over other things inside the house. I was searching professor's room and their I found a personal calendar diary of year "2048" and "THE PROJECT" written in bold letters on its cover. I picked it out from the book shelf that was placed mingled with some other professor's books as the diary was not placed properly like the way the other books were placed. It was placed between the two horizontally, there were couple of photographs glued to the first page of the diary and the title was written on it in bold letters in its first page, "THE UNIVERSE RECREATED".

I kept it secretly in my trousers pocket. I thought it might be having the information about the experiment or about which we have not got any clue. It was 4 A.M in the morning when we all get back to our base camps safely.

NEXT DAY

The case was closed. No one was harmed, and nothing was destroyed, but all his property of Collins Street was seized. The city was again filled up with the families living up there, the population has again filled up the city. The day was later named as 'BLACK DAY' in India.

After the work when I came back to my house in the morning, my wife came running to me hugged me tight and kissed me on my right cheek. She was crying badly. Her emotions were so deep that I just can't put those emotions in words. She hardly unwrapped her arms from my back and her head from my heart. I was silently crying in my heart without having any proof in my eyes.

Every family of a soldier, I think they all pray for our victory, which the whole country enjoys. But we do cry sometimes watching our family to be so much caring and that was all we expect from everyone in the country.

I kissed my son on his forehead who was sleeping when I arrived. That day changed me. Life has given a lesson to me. I thanked GOD looking at the locket which my wife was wearing. She was a religious soul while I was not before that day. Something made my tears to roll down by my cheeks when I was praying to the almighty. I begged him, cried by putting my knees down to forgive me for all the negative thoughts I was carrying from years.

After a short nap and the breakfast with my son. I was busy spending some quality time with him in the garden. My wife called out 'The Calendar Diary' which you have carried with you last night is here on the bed. I said okay.

After spending some time with him I got back to the living room to catch up the diary. It abruptly grabbed my attentions. I picked it up and so now the diary was with me in my hands. I opened it, stretching my back on the chair. On the very first page a photograph was glued over it on which 'love' was written. The photo was of a boy standing on beach having his beloved in his hands. On the second page when I turned it, there was written in bold letters 'PROJECT THE UNIVERSE RECREATED'.

THE CALENDER DIARY

The Valentine's Day

14-Feb 2049

The day was very special as it has its own importance having love in the air. I decorated the whole house with red lights, lily flowers, white curtains on window, red plain silk bedsheet with white pillows.

In the foots of the bed, I made a heart with candles following "I love you Anivesha", that was written by the candles below the heart giving it a more different look to make the mood for tonight. For today I made her to go out for shopping and planned to cook dinner for her by my own for the special night to make her feel more special.

I was following my dad's romantic steps of his time, when he proposed my mom to make her realize how much he loves her. He was more romantic, I think, I was just a follower and he was the guru of such love quotes and such steps to show how can we love more, specially to some special ones. I had read his personal diary which he wrote for mom, who was no more. But he never showed me his diary which he gifted my mom on her 31st anniversary. On which day one more year was added to my 18 years after my birth. He had mentioned their every beautiful memory and her beautiful pictures from her college days which they had never showed me. As It was their secret, their kissing selfies really had to be kept safe. He had expressed his every feeling from his locked heart whose key was my mom to weave his love in words.

This room was renewed for the first time after my mom and dad. The room was ready to wrap us, candles were ready to fill up the room with their awesomeness, bed was ready to hold the vibrations, and flowers were looking beautiful dangling in parts in the whole room. They were saying we are ready Mr. Ayan, and I was like, "No, how…. I am not prepared for this, right now". I was nervous and thinking why my dad had not written anything how to make love for first time or anything about intimacy.

Security camera recognized someone coming towards the door, and sends an image on my mobile, I checked, she was none other than Anivesha. She rang the bell continuously, but I was there looking her ranging the bell on my phone. On the fifth ring, I opened the door and she was like, why you got so late, baby. She hugged and kissed me there on the door step. I welcomed her, but I was nervous, super nervous not because of her, but because of our dinner date and love making this was all for first time love, intimacy, intercourse…

Well I managed everything, I managed myself not to behave like a nervous lover, after all 'I am my dad's son so how can I be nervous', such lines I had given to my mind to churn them for few hours to make him busy with them. And let my heart to play the rest of the role.

I had to show her calm, soothing and a very romantic me that day. I came out of me to follow my heart, to make her feel very special. Now it was the time for the dinner surprise for her. We came directly to the kitchen at the dining table, as she was already half an hour late. I took out a chair and offered her to sit, like I was the waiter serving her my hospitality. To plan something for her was the most beautiful part of my life. As every time she feels glad and very excited for the surprises. She was pleased to have such gratitude of mine that day. My change also did help her to be comfortable for our first valentine's day.

She said, 'thank you, thank you Ayan'.

Oh, please darling, it's all for you.

I took out another chair for me right in the adjacent space with her chair. I was about to serve the food, but she resisted my hand which was holding the plate, that I prepared to give her. She took the plate in her hand and served the food into the plates. I was surprised with her behavior. I had never thought her to be that kind of a girlfriend. But I felt blessed and lucky to have such an angel in my life.

She really appreciated my dinner and was glad to have me in that mood at least for that day. Every girl, I think wants to have a very romantic boyfriend who can make their at least first date special and romantic. She kissed on my cheek for that lovely dinner, it was her 2nd kiss in an hour time span. I didn't know how much wild she going to do tonight, but I was prepared for her wildness.

'Have you prepared all by yourself, Mr. Chef'. She asked.

Yes! Baby, I made it for you. I chuckled.

'Wow and that was more than I thought'. She said looking at clock on the front wall of her.

"Thank you". I said, putting a satisfactory smile on my face.

'Well you are a talented boyfriend, and it will help me too as I do not know how to cook'. She said smilingly brushing off her hands.

'I need you as my wife, not as a cook, baby'. I tagged her in this line, I didn't want to say, but it struck my heart and suddenly it popped up, which once I had read in a Facebook meme.

'Ohh, so sweet, but till when this offer is available Mr. Ayan'. She pointed out.

I started laughing, 'it will baby, till I will be in this world'. I love you, and this love will be increasing in my heart year by year. I hold her hand in mine and said to her looking into her eyes.

'I love you too'. She reciprocated.

The day was very special for both of us. We never thought of anything like this. But we did it. Because I think everything was planned and happening like it had to. Everyone has a story which is planned and would happen accordingly in parts. Our story would be a great example of that.

We stood up, I pulled her ardently, felt her warmth and comfy breaths as her lips were so closed to mine. My eyes didn't want to move their rotation and lips wanted to lick her lower sexy lip which was mind-blowing, as I was differently in love with her lips because of their extraordinary beauty. We kissed their standing in the kitchen pushing ourselves to the extreme innate feelings generated by our hormones to burn us in its eternity. She unstrapped her coat, suddenly I pushed her to the wall and hung her for minutes, kissed her desperately sliding her body up and down, forcing the wall to push again her hot body towards me for the newton's third law. I felt her to be more desperate than ever. I also unbuttoned my shirt, she started licking my chest and then again locked the lips. Her eyes were like they had been repeatedly saying that she wants to do the rest in the bed room. I got totally lost in her sexy body, my fingers were like they were playing a romantic song on her curvy figure. Then she smiled and whispered slowly biting my ear lope to go in the bed room. I held from her waist and uplifted her in my arms, she folded her legs and dropped her foot wears. Meanwhile she looked continuously into my eyes.

I softly unwrapped my arms from her body and let her to see the room. I switched on the red lights dangling from the ceiling and ignited the candles to burn orderly.

'WOW, the room is looking really adorable' she said.

I could figure out her emotions as she put her both hands on her mouth, to hide her emotions, she bended on her knees, her hands were still holding her emotions. She sat down at the floor in front of the beautiful-candle-scene.

'Ayan...' she murmured, and in a jiffy, she started crying. She loved that art of love made of candles 'A heart' followed by 'I Love You Anivesha'. She was sitting and crying near the bed where I made those words for her. I also sat there with her side, I slide myself closer to her, looked in her eyes. She was still crying. I could see the tears of love falling though her eyes.

'Aww Ayan'..., how do I put words to describe this delectable and amazing surprise'. She said looking into my eyes and in a very low and a crying tone. Her flattered lips, her crying eyes, her hands on her mouth were describing how beautiful it was. She was still crying.

I drew my lips closer to her and kissed her falling tear from her beautiful eyes. She started crying even more lovingly then.

'How is this Anivesha, isn't it beautiful'. I asked.

This is something that I had not even dream of, Ayan. And you showed me in the reality, which would have never possible without you to be with me. It's beautiful, it's just beautiful Ayan, thank you so much.

She was still crying, my surprise made her cry

Well wait, if you really want to thank me then wait.

What...? Do you still left with more surprises, she said with smile this time while tears were still rolling down her eyes?

I said 'yes', but the most beautiful surprise, you will be having at the midnight

Okay! Let's see, the midnight and you.

Just two hours left, and I couldn't wait anymore. She stood up and goes to the bed, comfort herself and called me like she was desperate for having the rest part of what the scene we had done in the kitchen. I didn't shut the door, as the house was just there after us. I powered the low led lights dangling romantically over the bed.

'Oh, another surprise', so you are ready today, mister...' she said and smiled.

I really liked the way she used to say me 'MISTER'.

She untied her red t-shirt and was signaling me by her fingers to come to her in seconds. I was standing searching my pocket for the condom packet.

'Yeah, I found it', I said to myself.

What, you found? She asked.

Wait, I am coming to show you. I said and grinned on my own.

I felt the smoothness of the silk bedsheet first, then I moved my fingers on her left leg and said, 'your legs are more smooth and sexy than this silk fabric', she laughed, hold my hand firmly and pushed me upon her body. She started kissing me again passionately but very slowly. I felt her completely, her wet lips and her tongue searching in me, love for her. I was totally lost in her, feeling her so closely on my body. Her heartbeats were also pounding but at less vibration as mine were. Her every touch had bringing a tingling sensation in my heart, second per second. And I was like begging her to pour more and more to fill hers' all love in me.

I Cuddled her tightly while sitting and on her back, I drew my name with my finger. We kissed. She relaxed properly back on the bed. I kissed down her at the sensitive part of her neck. I came down, felt her curvaceous breast. Every touch was bringing a pleasure in her. We kissed many times before, but the specialty of that day was making them more special. Soon we both got aroused and started feeling the moans and pleasures.

The midnight surprise,

5 minutes were left, and I was all prepared for my next surprise, the most beautiful of all. The fifth step written on my dad's diary having 5 stars on it. I hold her hand and looked in her eyes, we both were really very happy and little bit tired too now.

I said, 'I love you Anivesha' and hugged her, in a jiffy she prepared herself, put her legs upon my legs as I was taller than her. "So, Mr. Ayan where is my midnight surprise", She asked like a boss, looking into my eyes as now her eyes were in the same alignment as mine were. She wrapped me by her arms and slowly bit my lower lip in excitement.

I started walking holding her there. I stepped up on the ladder with her, Kissed her many times in the way to the roof. She said, 'I really loved the way you love'. I winked and brushed by my nose to her tip to tip.

We came to the roof. she was shocked to see the set for that night which I prepared for her on the terrace. I arranged a big sized couch in the balcony. Her favorite flowers, her favorite music to give a little more softness to the night which we had to spend sitting and remembering all our beautiful memories of our beautiful days.

We both sat down on the couch in the balcony below the black foreground of the sky with tingling stars to make it more delectable. We relaxed back properly. I folded my left arm below my head. She came closer and put her chin on my chest looked into my eyes. She wrapped me firmly by her right hand, closed her eyes and rested her head down on my chest.

'I am very happy today. My life before you were like a hell boring, just passing. But a spark I got and that is you Anivesha. I don't know what would be in my life if you hadn't accepted my love'. I said looking up the sky.

'For me you are also like that spark, which you mentioned for me, Ayan. And even I am pleased to have you as my boy, and I am very excited to live my rest of the life with you'. She said and hold me very tightly. I could feel the emotions of love, to what nothing sands in this world.

We both left our self-there and we started talking about our beautiful past. We smiled, laughed, remembering our meetings, our celebrations. That night conjured over both of our minds and hearts. We were lost in the eternity of that delectable quality time with each other.

AYAN

My mom was a physics professor. One day, when she was coming from her work, it was raining. She was in a taxi, coming home after the work. The breaks of the taxi did not work due which it loses its control and the taxi stroke on the divider, further the taxi fell from the fly over to the under passing highway and my mom's and the driver's dead body lying there, blood flowed out after having mixed up with rain water which drenched the road with blood.

My dad had lost all his hopes from the life, whose dreams of giving his dreams which he has written for mom to give her happiness and her awaited surprises. He was totally shattered after that accident. Even for weeks he had not believed us. He gave up on everything. I remember, I saw my strength to be broken down that day. He was my strength. He supported me and my mom at every aspect of life.

I joined the masters cum Ph.D. course, where I met with the most beautiful girl Anivesha. I didn't know whether she was that kind of beautiful or not but what my heart's status was, she was. Who hardly resisted himself in getting distracted for her. Why not, even to die for her for what she gave me was not sufficient to even equal her love for me. In the second year, I was totally engaged with my studies. I gave all of me towards physics as like for always it has attracted me towards its concepts on why, what, and how.

After completing the bachelor's degree from the forks university, in whose company my dad worked and because of which the university offered free education to me as my dad was a senior scientist, he discovered new formulas for their medical issues. He was an expert in nucleic and biological processes. He was working on the formula of making a cell or a whole tissue invisible.

I had scored well and so got a golden chance to pursue MSC and PHD degree like once my father had persuaded from the 'Quantum University'. The best university for the higher education, which selects only 10 thousand of students from all over the world after getting cleared with two ordeal and lengthy written exams, medical tests and interviews.

ONE-EYE-GAP-LOOK

23rd April 2048

I pressed the button on the electric automated bus to get off at the 'selvis phase-II' bus stop. It was in one of the coolest and the beautiful city of Bangalore. The streets were crowded day and night. We always provided flexibility in our life style to keep moving in the chaos that has been created by us in the race of survival. This city could be the best example of it.

I with my laptop started heading towards the entrance of the college, took out my handkerchief from the pocket to clean my oily skin before I get noticed by someone with an oil producing factory on my face. The road was busy with a normal heavy traffic fighting with the friction of their tires.

There was no one at the main gate, as I was already 20 min late. There was a hotel 7 sky in the adjacent space of the university. The city was one of the most hectic places in Bangalore. It was at its center and the main hub for education and technology.

I held my e-card to the censor to get an application letter for my third year of graduation to get all the documents and details about the class. 'This card is expired', the computer declined my e-card saying this line. What, expired, I asked to myself, looking down at the card holding it in my right hand and searching for another one in the bag for the first-year e-card. Valid for only 2 years was written on its back side. I put it back in the bag. Again, tried the same card once again but the same sound again pierced through my ears.

'Excuse me',

I heard a familiar voice but this time not of any Computer to make another declination of my request. I turned around and let her to do it first. It was a female voice, I did not look at her, just got turned and started looking at the e-card, 'what wrong could be with the card,' I turned to her but her face was not clear as she was standing showing only her butts and black hair with a very cute blonde hair cut, no lipstick but they were glowing perhaps some lip glow was applied in order to protect them, no heels, just a simple t-shirt with blue Levis old fashioned jean. She turned to ask time, she was wearing her own wrist watch but she asked me, perhaps her watch have stopped. 9:30 I said, she looked into my eyes for the answer in back, she looked like she wanted to say something more with those beautiful eyes to me, what I thought standing, looking her while telling her the time. And I looked her very deeply and those 5 seconds, were like I was looking her from hours continuously. Her hairs were falling over her face giving a little gap to her eye to look at my slow motioned lips telling her nnnnnniiiiineeee ttthhhhhiiiirrrttyyyyyy.

That slow time zone was very strange to me, because before her, I had never noticed any of from thousands of girls ever before like that. Her e-card was accepted and now she was having her details in her hands. Now for again this was my chance. I did the same again, held the e-card on the censor and waited for it to say the card has been expired. In the mean time I looked back cleverly to see her again, she was standing there reading her details. Her hairs were still falling over her cute face. She didn't look at me even once. But I kept my eyes glancing on her. Looking her like I saw her for the first time. Which was not true I thought?

Had I seen her before?

Ohh Yes,

what?

She is in my class.

Ohh really!

Riya, um pray no, nikanshi…. Ohhno,

I was asking my lazy mind to answer her name. But like always it says that he had not any interest in learning any girls' name. I know why have answered me that, because my mind never got any command of learning such names from my heart as I have never fallen for anyone before.

"The card was damaged but is cleared for now, get the new card for the next entry soon," Someone said me giving my details by his hand extending it out of the small opening below the censor. 'Okay sir', I replied and turned, she was reading her details. When I walked away some steps ahead, she asked me to wait for her. I stopped. I was frozen for that second and heart had started making chaos in the chest like if he wanted to say, 'let me come out, let me come out'.

I was just walking along her side, looking her secretly. I didn't have such guts or feelings at that time to ask her name or to start a chitchat there. I was just walking silently, like a kid following his father on teacher's day meeting. Neither in my bachelor's nor in my two years of Master's, studying with the same girl in the same class, I hardly felt comfortable in walking with her alone, I was missing motu, to give me his company. That day I realized that really, I was a Dumbo which was my nickname. Not given by dad or mom, my classmates had   glued it to me. I didn't like this name to be called out by someone. But what could I do with an abrupt attachment.

Hello Ayan,

Finally, she extended her left hand forward to wave with my right hand. I was looking at my details thinking about motu, how he got up early today and reached on time.

I had been walking lost in somewhere deep in my thoughts and after a jiffy, my eye balls got their movement to target her soft hand. I turned my head slowly towards her hand. She was wearing a black color band and a wrist watch. I touched her soft skin while holding it.

'Hi…Priya', I said. But the answer for her name was not sure, it was a doubt.

I forgot to undo the process of handshake. I was very nervous for that slow time zone. I kept holding her hand and I was looking at my details walking with her, falling every second softy on her.

"Anivesha" she said,

I brought my tongue down in between my teeth and hit it hard. She grinned over my silly reply.

'What, not Priya…,' I reacted like a thief, got caught red-handed for his crime.

She laughed and uttered very softly 'it's ok'

'Nice name', I will remember it for every next time. I said smilingly in a shy tone.

That time my heart has also commanded to my brainless brain to fix it in a very special space.

She was still laughing looking at me. I was looking on the way. I was thinking for hers' such an apt smile. I turned to see her, what had happened for what she had ben grinning secretly? I remember, I was walking still holding her hand from the way I held it. And perhaps she was grinning upon this. I suddenly undo my hand and put it in my pocket, felt her hand's warmth by clenching the fist, brushed my fingers inside the pocket and smiled for myself.

I took out the handkerchief again to clean out my face. We walked into the campus, searched for the classroom. And that beautiful but quite informal time zone got finished.

I don't know what had happened to me. I was not satisfied by the handshake or by her one-eye-gap-look. I wanted more. I wanted to talk to her. I wanted to tell her about me. I wanted her heart also to feel the same for me.

I was looking at her in the classroom for few minutes perhaps to expect an apt answer from her or to satisfy the need of my heart. She was busy reading something on her mobile phone sitting on the next bench to mine. I was like a guy who will settle his dick down even after an offer from a sexy pussy and will not fuck her. I was like a guy who had very few friends on Facebook and most of them were those whom I did not know or else I was more interested to work on physics principle, music and playing guitar. I had not even noticed her for the last 2 years of my graduation. Perhaps she did, as she had my name in her memory. My mind got distracted couldn't say what was all that. But something has happened very strange for which there was a very long fight with my mad heart and my genius mind. I let her to ruin my heart or can say, I didn't have any other better solution for it.

Well I remember I was still looking at her, irrespective of other students in the class. Abruptly, she turned, perhaps I had not noticed her looking and smiling at my weird activities. I can't resist myself to not to peep at her. I was looking at her continuously. Abruptly she looked at me. I turned my head suddenly with the speed of bullet when I came back in my nerves. I got confused what to do after getting caught at such situations. I just turned myself and due to a sudden reflex action, my leg got stuck between two desks, my pen dropped, the notes had fallen down. I stood up to give a gap between them to relax my leg back. She was laughing hardly, on how I was doing the things with me.

That was really a very embarrassing moment for me, as she caught me red handed looking at her. Who knows what my intentions were. On that day I looked at her very carefully.

Before today she was also like any other girl for me, to whom I hadn't preferred to give any of my attentions. Even she was a very simple girl. She was wearing old fashioned clothes but was looking extraordinarily beautiful. I don't know why people for whom you fall in love became very important and exclusively beautiful. There were many beautiful girls in the campus after her, but only for her, my heart felt safe to get distracted and this has happened to me for the first time.

NEXTDAY

Next day, I reached the college at the same time where we met yesterday. I again reached late so to meet her again there for today too. I wanted to hold her hand and again wanted to travel the same corridors of the college with her. I didn't know whether she will be again late for today or not, but my heart was saying, she would. So, for my heart's sake I followed him and got late.

I didn't know why she was still roaming from my heart to mind inside my veins. Why I, missed her last night. Why I was thinking of her while coming to the college.

I waited for her, sitting in the outer park of the college. I was thinking of what special have happened yesterday, to which I was glued, to which I was thinking madly upon. There were umpteen questions, my mind was asking while sitting there that "why I am sitting here not going into the class room even after getting so late", and the answer was very simple, "for her", I said shamelessly. As now my heart had taken over the command for all other questions and action. I looked at the main gate to check if she came or not, then I looked at my watch to check the time. It was 10:30 and the class must be started by now. I got panicked and the mood got off by itself. I was about to stand to walk by the side of the park to follow the corridors alone in disappointment. In that half standing posture, I saw her moving away from me going towards the class room without even noticing me. She had plugged her earphone in her ears. I looked back again at the main gate to replicate how and when she came and gone. And why she had not even noticed me sitting here. I hurried my legs to move faster to get in tune with her. I stopped, when she turned after noticing me. She unplugged her earphone and leaned towards me, extended her hand to brush it with mine.

"HI…" she said with the same cute smile on her face, then she looked back the way I came running to her. she asked why you were running? I know it may be late but look at you, your face got drenched with sweat. Don't worry the class will start at around 11 perfectly, so why to hurry. It was around 50 meters when I missed her.

It's okay! How are you? I asked.

She smiled and said 'AWESOME'.

For her that AWESOME, I wanted to tell her that I was waiting and standing tiredly now, what I was feeling for her from the single minute since I saw her. I wanted to hold her again and to spend the whole day with her, holding her in my lap. She unleashed me from my virtual dreams. I realized that my friends were somehow right in attaching that nickname with my attitude. I thought, really, I was DUMBO in attracting someone or in talking to a girl. We both hurried and reached the classroom.

I was surprised why she came to sit here. There were lots of vacant seats in the class, so why she chooses this seat. I thought, when she came into the class with me and chosen the adjacent seat next to me although the seats were separated by a wide space but were adjacently connected.

'This seat is because this is the perfect space to get the clear view of the projector', my mind answers this useless answer to me.

'Well not like that, what you are saying, it might be because of the possibility that she wants herself in a comfortable space, and with Ayan she has her comfortableness', my heart answered in contrast, which satisfied me without any apt reason for my restlessness.

For the new session as students were less so most of the benches at the back were vacant and I was sitting on the last bench in the rightmost row. As I was used to sitting at the back of the class, where hardly someone would pay his weird attentions on me and thus, the back space was all time perfect for me. I was with her or can say so close that I was breathing her comfy breaths, she was exhaling in the amid space between her and me or it might be 'the love effect'. That cozy feeling in the heart somewhere was soothing my last night pain of missing her. In that small section of the space of the class between her seat to mine, I was feeling her closeness towards me. She was somewhere attracting me towards her. I couldn't resist myself any more. I was dying every second looking at her secretly.

'Hello, Anivesha', I said, as I was very frantic to start the chitchat with her. I wanted to untie her all the thoughts she had. I wanted to unwrap her from herself on me. When I was with her in the corridors in the morning, I was missing motu to give his company. But fortunately, he was absent that day, and to peep into her matter I was liberal. If he would have with me, then definitely would have asked, 'why was I looking at her'?

She was sitting alone and no her friend, if she had had any were there was a blank seat. My heart was pondering on how I should start a conversation with her. There was some time to start the class. So, I drew my inner me, that was feeling safe with her out of me. And prepared to bombard a sweet conversation with her to spend some quality time together.

'Do you have any extra pen?' I completely leaned over her desk and asked, brow creased and a pseudo force came out to pull me to get back to the spot again.

'Yes sure', she replied and leaned towards me to give it.

'Thanks, Anivesha', I giggled and get back to the seat again.

She again turned and asked,

'Ohh so, you have remembered my name', She grinned and put forward a beautiful smile to start a contented chat, which could be continued.

I smiled back, I slide my butts to the other nook of the seat.

'Can I ask you something', I asked confidently.

She turned towards me, putting her right elbow on the armrest of the seat and came closer to me.

'yes sure', she said smilingly.

'Eh, actually I don't know, should I ask you that or not', my mind screamed from inside to put a sensual answer to a senseless me.

But my heart put forward his statement and satisfied me.

I summoned up myself to ask her, 'why didn't you waited for me'? when I was waiting for you in the park. Cutting the time uprooting the green brushes there.

"Sorry", but perhaps, I didn't have noticed you. She replied in a flash.

'Ohh, but I was there'. I said like an innocent kid in a very sweet tone, breaking the eye contact, looking at my books. I made myself busy opening and closing the cap of the pen which she gave me by my left hand to show my restlessness upon waiting for her.

A silence was settled for few seconds, I was thinking while looking at my books what she might be thinking as she has not uttered a single word after that. I looked up at her. She was also looking at me and grinning.

'Why were you waiting, mister, BTW'. She asked and broke the silence between us.

I blushed off. What to say now, why I was waiting for her. I smiled at her, just smiled and slide myself away from her to the other nook of the seat.

She turned, and I thanked GOD as the class was started. I didn't want to answer her for that weird question.

After the college I got into the metro after her, following up to the way she was going. The rush was as usual very busy inside the metro and I didn't want to lose her from my sight for even a second. I tried hard to put my jaw back to my mouth to follow her. I had struggled between the butts and the bloated tummies floating and blocking my way after her. I had to grab a space in adjacent to her. Finally, she stopped and so was I. She looked at the black window glass of the metro, which was showing my reflection. She looked at it, grinned, thought, adjusted her hairs at the right which were falling over her left eye by her left hand and looked at me by that one-eye-gap-look. Her hairs were so naughty that whenever she adjusted her hairs from her left eye, soon they slip to fall over again. Making one-eye-gap-look.

Soon after stopping at one of the busy station. We get to sit and yes, I was at her side. We didn't talk yet. But I think she was not bothered from my apt activities. Even I couldn't believe myself doing all that, which I had never thought to do.

'And now, the high time you should start pointing out some hidden questions and feelings', my heart accelerated me from inside to talk to her.

I wanted to ask many things about her, I wanted to tell a lot about myself to her. Some pseudo forces from the left side of my chest had started arousing me.

I summoned up my first line to start, yes to ignite an intimate desire to burn myself with her. I was not sure that those feelings were love or not. But something was there that pushing me towards her or pulling me towards her. I didn't want to let her go. I had never felt such a desperate feeling ever before her.

She was sitting silently, looking at her Left and right. I thought she was feeling comfortable with me. So, there would be no problem to try my luck for that beauty.

When I was about to start the talk. she looked, and asked 'where do you live?' I think she was more absorbed in me than I was in her. As at every chance she put forward a question not me.

'Collins street', I said her so laud enough, for which she did ask it again,

Sorry, she excused.

Collins street, I said again in an audible voice, after clearing my throat.

'And you?' I questioned back.

'Mantra' she said.

Eh, next to Collins street, I said smugly.

Yeah! Next to Collins street.

She too started smiling, but what for? Well I did so because I got my girl near my locality where I could go with a 15 min walk but why she laughed?

'Because, your abrupt reaction made her to make a face to crinkle and smile'. My mind said complacently.

'Noooo…O, she also likes you and thus she smiles', my heart stated back again and did hold over the situation and yes, it was right again. 'She does like me, she does like me'. I insanely accepted that.

You seem very much excited today, aren't you? she questioned.

'well not so special but yeah, I do also feel something-something in this day, I said.

What something-something…? She asked.

First, I smiled, why do girl have to ask everything, and boys have to understand everything. They want their answer for their every question and we boys, we just make ideas "ohh, yes she talked to me, she is showing her interest". And all like that.

I am very happy to get myself applicable for the third year. To get into this college was my dream when I was in class 12. I had passed the second year with good marks. So just…, I said. I knew the answer was a kinky one but beside it, I had not any.

'Ohh, this is your something-something. Well you had planned your future so nicely. But I was not sure that I will also be able to study here or not, but look, it was fortune that I am here. She said smilingly.

What would you like to do if this had not happened to you? I asked.

'I would have killed myself', she shocked me, and soon started laughing on it.

I thought she yelled the joked, I too started insanely tuning my teeth with hers'.

'Ok, can we meet tomorrow but in the college bus. We could come along the way'. She asked.

'Yes, why not'. I replied with a tone of joy in my voice. As I stood up to leave her out at my station, we bid goodbyes to each other.

See you tomorrow, I said from between the sliding doors. I could not hear her 'yes sure' but I have fantasized it.

INCOMPLETE KISS

Next day

The smart window system helped the curtains to pass the sunlight through the window glass. The window was photo sensitive and when the sunrays fall on it, the curtains slides away by themselves. It works as an alarm system. They all slide away and let the sun rays to hit on my head and eyes. The room was filled with the yellowish beautiful natural light. Soon after the alarm clock have started hitting my unconscious mind to wake me up. I dragged the bedsheet, moved from one side of the bed to the other, untie my night blinker. Murmured hmm… in a lazy tone. Stretched my left hand from under the pillow and hit it to the alarm clock to shut its piercing sound. When I tried for few times to do so without my eyes in action, the clock fell on my head and then I realized the new morning arrived. I picked the clock and checked the time by my one opened eye as other was still sleeping.

It was 9:30 'W-T-F', I abruptly stood up from the bed. Went to the kitchen gulped a glass of water, refreshed myself, bathed properly. I didn't want to get late and to reach the college from the different bus. She had promised to be on time to go to the college through the College bus. I sprayed some delectable fragrance to impress her. After the breakfast sorry but only the milk with boiled eggs, I came out to catch the bus. It would have arrived at 10:00 a.m. I used to live alone after my mom and dad. My uncle did not want me to live with them, so I shifted from their house and started living alone in my dad's house.

I was waiting under the street light pole outside my house where the bus stop was. I prepared myself in a while, when the bus was at around 50 meters. I adjusted my watch by my right hand. I flipped my head in forward direction and adjusted the hairs by the fingers to their perfect position. Now I was ready to enter the bus. In amid time between its applying the brakes to the time it had stopped, I looked up through the window to catch Anivesha. She was also looking at me when I was standing, waiting for the bus to stop. She smiled and waved at me through the window pane. I smiled back and entered the bus. Finally, I was in and so my heart started beating fast as if it wanted to say something or as it was very excited to talk. I saw an empty seat next to her. She was still looking out of the window at my house. Perhaps she might be looking how beautiful, my house was. Well for that I think it wasn't. I picked forward my laptop bag from the back and put it down and sit there along her side. She extended her hand to shake with mine.

I said, 'hello Anivesha'.

Hi… Ayan, how are you?

I am fine and you,

'Me too'. She said and gave me her first smile of the day. She welcomed me with her cute smile and so my lips got wider and smiled back to her. She again turned her head outside of the window. I too turned to look what she was looking. She turned inward but abruptly while I was still looking outside, and her lips got touched to my cheeks. A thunder of feeling ran out of me that moment.

She whispered 'ohh I am sorry', but didn't smiled over it as it seemed to be happened accidentally for which neither she was prepared nor was I. I didn't even answer her back but felt really happy for that touch, a smile came by its own. Today I noticed her lips to be glittered with lipstick whose imprint was now at my cheek. I brushed it off by my fingers and then I replied, 'it is okay'.

What were you looking out of the window? I asked.

'Your house', She replied slowly looking down at her bag. She was still feeling uncomfortable with that incomplete kiss.

Ohh, I know Anivesha, it was an accidental, please forget it, and if someone has to feel sorry for that, it should be I not you, so please forget it, I am sorry, I said.

You need not to be sorry Ayaan, let's forget it. She said smilingly, looking keenly in the deepness of my eyes. She really liked the way I understood and caressed her, she liked the way I pampered her.

'Your house looks so old', she asked.

Yeah, it is. Well it will be a very long story if I start telling you. I said to her feeling sad for the house, that had not been even repainted or even washed properly. Its garden was like a graveyard outside my house.

Ohh, so it is, okay but promise you will tell it to me some other day, she said.

Sure, I assured her that I will narrate my story to her. She was looking very beautiful in her dress and her blonde hairs were the fabulous part of her delectable beauty. She had a habit of shaking her right leg while sitting and so she was shaking. And at some time, during her leg's vibrations they were touching mine, its peak value and I smiled for her such an apt behavior. She would stop shaking her legs when she notices me smiling on her and soon after it start again by itself. I did let her do what she was doing and irrespective of other students who themselves were busy with their love life in the bus. I looked at her and many times when I didn't, she looked at me. About half an hour of quality time we spent in the bus. We talked about what was going on or what we will be doing up to. Nothing so crispy that could produce some more tingling sensation in me.

Outside the college after getting off from the bus. I saw Motu coming towards me. Who was the only one after Anivesha with whom I could feel comfortable.

He cuddled me, and asked 'oye ye kon hai', who she is? in a very sarcastic way close to my ear, after looking Anivesha standing at my back waiting for me to go.

Well Anivesha he is Nikansh and Nikansh she is Anivehsa.

I introduced them to each other. I knew Motu would think what she was doing with me. But I did let the suspense of Anivesha to be a suspense for him, as I had a very less faith on him to digest such things.

MOTU

Motu was my best friend and more he was like my brother, younger brother, he was one year younger than me. Well it was right I am mentioning him as Motu, but if he would get to know about it he will be angry. Except me, all the boys from the class used to call or tease him by this nickname Motu, and they called him like, 'Oye Motu'. Well do not think I did not had any courage to say him Motu. I didn't like that name indeed, that's why for me Nikansh is better than 'Motu'.

But he was a genius in computer and had a potential to hack someone's account and to delete it just like uprooting it from its existence. For which he has also helped other student in their projects. His intelligence and passion about coding and networks was very widespread among the senior students too. Once I asked him from where he learnt all that as he was pursuing physics honors with me not the computer science. His answer was, he learnt the basics from his dad when he was just 12 years old, he could have hacked the websites and more he learned by himself studying from the books and internet. That had really impressed me when I met him.

When we entered the class, I wanted to go to the row where Anivesha was going but as Motu was with me. We sat at the back bench in the right most row. She sat in the next row to mine. She was perfectly visible to me, but I was not to her. The seat next to her was empty but as Motu insisted, I had no choice.

Why this love has happened to me. Did I wish it to fall in my life? NO, I didn't, rather I hated those who were engaged in those love triangles. There was only one triangle that controlled me and that was my 'physics honors, music and my secret life of living as a secret'. Since those days, I think we all are to be loved by someone. Someone whose presence make you feel what you hadn't felt with others, someone whose absence can make you numb over what you are, someone who keeps loving you till you are or till your love is alive. I had never believed in love before, but Anivesha made me to feel it, to taste it for her. Her brown eyes had always seduced me in their softness and the love they had wrapped deep inside.

I had been studying in the class but not like I had been before her. I started looking at her most of the time when I got some free time. She began attracting me more. But I didn't want to lose my chapters and concepts during the class just to look her. But it became very difficult for me to turn a as a simple Ayan who would hardly look at her. So, I just peeped at her leisurely, hadn't changed completely to be a day dreamer for her.

She had also turned her head many times to make out her glances at me. I just simply smiled didn't react further to her changed behavior. I was totally sure that she too started liking me. Thanks to the yesterday's absence of Motu, as he had not asked me till, why she was smiling and looking at us turning back many times.

Motu lives in the south of selvice, while my route was at the north. So, during the departure after Motu, I have always kept myself busy with Anivesha. I didn't want to tell Motu about it.

So, after Motu left, I got back to the bus where Anivesha might be waiting and I was right, she looked at me when I entered the bus. The seat next to her was kept vacant. I smiled at her look and thanked her about that pleasure within my heart. I can't tell or describe what my feelings were. It was happening like I had written her in my story to do as like as I wanted her to do for me. Things were happening in perfect manner to make a perfect story. The universe seemed like it is busy in building up a new space for the storm of love that was taking birth day by day for me and I think for her too. I thanked god for this beautiful gift and I did pray not to let her go away from my destiny.

I sat on that vacant seat, 'Sitting with her was like to ride on high waves of Heart beats for my heart and a positive aura for my mind.

Hello, did you wait for me? I asked her to clear my temptation about the question.

"No", she giggled over my silly question. And her blunt reply of "NO" have passed through the ears to my heart. It made me to think whether, 'she likes me or not'. Her answer hit my heart like a sharp pointing knife have stabbed in it.

'Ohh...'then I might be the wrong person to sit here'. I said in a tone of disappointment with my crinkled brow and rushed to sit at the back seat. I thought that she will stop me by herself. But no, she had not stopped me, she had not even smiled or looked back to give me a single hint.

When the bus was filled, I silently moved to that seat again. I was helpless. I had to go. My heart aroused me. When I sat on the vacant seat next to her, she looked at me and smiled. I didn't react this time. My heart was frowned. Who was madly in love with her.

'I didn't have reserved the seat, but 'why you left it?' she grinned and questioned. These eccentric questions were the most unanswerable questions for me. I couldn't tell her directly about my fidgetiness. I wanted to tell her after when she would assure me that she too like me. if I would have told her, perhaps the story might be twisted. So, I decided to wait for the destiny to turn the next page of our love to be as slowly as it wanted.

I didn't answer her back rather I started smiling. Smiling, because she was right, if she had not reserved the seat then, why I had left the seat?

That was so childish act of you Ayan. She said smugly.

I loved the way she pointed out an act of me. Though it was childish but was so lovely when she said to me. It was something like if someone's girlfriend challenged him to eat red chilies in love and he did not feel and over react to its chilliness. Love makes you to love those things too to which you had never pay your attentions before.

So, when you will be telling your story? she asked. I thought it to be a perfect changer for my story, to get her closer to me.

'The coming Sunday', I said confidently with a sarcastic smile.

Smart hmm…Well okay let's meet tomorrow.

'Oh' thank you. But really, I didn't know that tomorrow is a Sunday, it was random. I crinkled.

Your number? I asked to continue the flow.

She shared her number and my fingers followed the pattern on my dialing screen and I saved it as Anivesha.

I didn't think my love story to be so easy and so skipping. That was just happening, I was not controlling but something like love in between was controlling us. True love or the first love made you feel the awesomeness of it.

I bid goodbye at my stop, see you tomorrow. I smiled but she was busy in looking at my house. I flattered my hand to get her attention even I jumped, finally she smiled back and waved at me by her hand taking it out of the window.

Same day,

My heart was satisfied. Finally, my cell phone felt proud having her number saved in its contact list. I had pinned it on the top.

I was very happy that day. Smile was coming on its own. I looked myself in the mirror many times to adjust my hairs with some classy styles. I have also tried to swipe her number to the right to make a call, but soon I slide it back on the left and cancelled it every time. The day time had passed in sliding her number to the right and to the left.

At 9:00 p.m.

After the dinner I logged in Facebook, searched her, send her friend request, she accepted as she was online that time.

Her profile pic was just 'wow'. Firstly, I reacted on it by a heart emoji. I felt a tingling sensation soon after that.

'Adorable,' I commented.

'Thank you', soon a reply was added.

But she had just put a thumb on my comment. I thought it to be the beginning, beginning of the next page of our story.

'Hi… ', I sent a message.

Hlw ☺, she replied.

What are you doing? I asked.

Nothing much, just going to bed.

You sleep so early; do you have to wake up early? I asked.

No, 😆😆😆…, actually I used to sleep early, and I used to wake up late. She replied.

'Ohh', you are dreamer. I pointed out.

No, I am sleeper, 😆😆😆. She chuckled.

Well, good. I said. But I was thinking why she needed to sleep too much. She was prudent, how does she manage all this?

I cuddled my pillow and had stretched myself on the bed, lied straight, I switched off the lights by the cellphone and I was at the apex of my excitement.

Do you really want to know about me? I asked.

'Well not, I want to know about your house, which seems so weak'. She again shattered my excitement. Then I thought girls like to make things rounder and twisted. I smiled over her that silly reply through which she had been trying to show her no interest in me. Soon I replicate her memories in which she had perfectly mentioned that yes, she too likes me. I smiled over and over again.

Eh, yes, ok I will tell you tomorrow about it. I said.

Type, 'I like you' my heart pressed my nerves from inside. But how could I, just two days had passed. I reminded him.

So, don't you like her? 'Eh' he asked smugly.

Yeah, I do.

So, tell her,

No,

Yes,

No no,

Yes, yes ☹

No, and it is final. I said.

Go-to-hell… he frowned and replied.

So, how would be CCD to meet, I asked.

Nice, I was also thinking about it. She replied.

'Okay' but do promise… I typed.

What...?

You will be definitely coming.

☺ yes, I will. She assured me.

Okay, good night, hope I didn't bothered your sleep. I said.

She laughed, 'NO', you not. Goodnight and sweet dreams. She said.

After her, her "sweet dreams" compelled me to think on it. Does she also know that my dreams will get higher and beautiful thoughts after talking to her? Does she had an idea that she will be coming in my dreams. I smiled, put the pillow down my neck, shut my eyes by the blinker and had gone to sleep in her "Sweet Dreams".

THE CAFÉ COFFEE DAY

At CCD,

I wanted that day to be special for us. It was just informal meeting yet I thought to put on some classy outfit to look classy. I put on my white shirt with dark blue jean and a blazer. I was looking completely what I was not, "handsome". I thought she would be impressed.

I was waiting at the corner table in the CCD with a little bit nervousness on my face for what she would think after I tell my story to her. I was thinking about my apt story. I wanted that date to be totally out of my story. But I was compelled because she only liked to hear about my house, not about me. I knew if I will start telling my story, she wouldn't let me to flirt with her or my heart would stop by itself.

I wanted to say her that yeah, "I like you". Moreover, I wanted to tell all about me, but for that she needed to arrive fast. I was sitting near the window seat in the right corner so that I could get her view from the glass.

The wait was over, I saw her coming, I smiled and prepared myself instantly. Heartbeats increased. I was happy as a smile I could feel on my face came on its own, but something had been worried inside and that was my heart.

"Wow", I looked at her and my heart screamed insanely. She was wearing a red top with low waist dark blue jeans. If you have loved someone, then you will be having your idea 'how much beautiful she was looking to me'. She entered and rolled her eyes around in the café to find me.

Hi, here. I drew her attention. I was about two tables away from her.

She smiled and started coming closer. My heart had skipped its beats and got lost in her. I was spell-bound by her beauty.

'Looking nice', Ayan.

She plugged in her first line to start up the talk and I loved the way she called out my name.

Thank you, I blushed, more I was at the apex of feeling special for her.

'You too, the pretty girl and your hairs are just beautiful'. I said relaxing myself at the back of the couch. There were two couches and a robotic arm in between them which was capable of cleaning the raw stains by itself. While relaxing myself back to the sofa, I checked the time in the phone. I put it back and leaned forward exactly like I was sitting earlier. I forgot to pick my wrist watch while coming.

Ohh, thank you. She replied.

Which coffee, would you like to have? I asked.

'Well, hmm...' after few minutes of hmm.

Cold one, finally she replied.

'What the fuck', I like hot coffee, order cold for her and hot for yourself and after all firstly love yourself' my mind had put his wish of what he likes, the cold one or the hot one.

'No, she is a girl and not only the girl, she is special. And after all you do love her Ayan, so how could you only love yourself? Order what she want'. This was my heart's opinion and like always it had satisfied me this time also.

'Go-to-hell, ASSHOLE'. My mind abused my sweet heart.

'Eh', Same-to-you. Heart replied insanely.

Well these were my two characters that satisfied me at my every situation, my heart and my brain.

'Hmm, two cold coffees vegan shake', finally I put the command on the tablet that has been installed in the robotic arm to take the orders of the customers.

'Just 15 minutes sir', the computer replied.

Okay, so what do you wanted to ask? I questioned her.

'About your house and I didn't agree just to discuss the house matter'. She smiled and said in a little bit shy tone. I thought last light, when she said, 'not about me, but she wanted to know about the house only' and now she was saying that she does not only want to discuss about the house. What does she mean?

'Eh', I was about to say, okay. But she continued.

'I was alone from months. I didn't have any coffee or any dinner outside Just to repair my taste I agreed for your company'. She said.

Ohh, that's nice. Actually, I too need someone's company to go to such places. You know the couple or good friends usually used to come here. I said.

Yes…she murmured sadly with crinkled face.

But, I promise I will give you my company and we will have fun with each other, 'friends'. I extended my hand to get an answer in back and to make her comfortable with me.

She held my hand and agreed "yes, friends".

'Well okay', first have your coffee it is here. I said after looking at robot coming to put our order there. That was before the time, it came only in 10 minutes.

I was thinking from where I should start, I have a lot of pain beside my happiness. I have suffered a lot. I too wanted someone's shoulder on which I can flood out my tears of the pain I have suffered.

'So, Anivesha, please promise first that you will not leave till I finish back my life story'.

I said looking into her eyes. She was sipping the coffee. After sipping, she put her cup down and moved her left hand on mine, brushed over it, slowly to assure me.

'Yes, I will', she looked in my eyes and assured me.

5:15 P.M., first round of coffee.

Well Anivehsa life was not easy and simple with me as like it has been with others. I have seen many ups and downs and many problems in my life. It was 23rd September 2044, when my mom died in an accident. I started telling my story from beginning to her.

"Dr. John brij", have you heard this name? I asked.

"Yes", she leaned forward and with curiosity and replied, 'who doesn't know about this nifty and great scientist Dr. John brij, 'the man who succeeded in reducing the size of the tissue'.

'Yeah, after a jiffy I said, "He was my father".

Her jaw had fallen to her breast, she had covered her mouth by her hands and her eyes were about sink into the tears up to the brim.

'I am sorry', she said.

Have your coffee Anivesha, I have told you that the story is quite long.

'No….no…. its ok please carry on'. She wanted to hear more about my pains.

So, after my mom, dad felt loneness and depressed. He loved her very much, even more than his experiments, more than his success and more than anything else.

Once when I came back to home after 3 months of my mom's death. I was in Mumbai doing my schooling there. Those days, I remember he used to say, 'I want to go where you are, I want to go where you are…'very insanely looking at her photographs. I had tried my best to hold him, to take him out of his situation. I saw many times dad always used to talk about a project, about to create a new universe, about to create his own algorithms of life, to get my mom with him. His believe was that 'everyone should have equal life time span' so that the pain of losing someone you love will not be so much. He wanted to create his own life where he can live as many years, as many ages he wanted.

He wrote a theory in which he mentioned this life to be a game of algorithms and some kind of programs. He wanted to create one such program which could create my mom again, which could create her life, her memories again.

'Waooooohh, what…? he was just amazing'. She said, with her bloated face with so much curiosity. She forgot to even sip her coffee. She was also a physics prudent student thus she could able to design the deepness of the theory I was discussing with her.

Her curiosity was right at which level it was because, yes, my dad wanted to bring out his biggest invention of all the time. PROJECT- THE UNIERSE RECREATED. In which he wished to create my mom's life again.

6:30 P.M., 2nd round of coffee.

Yes, he was like that. I said and offered another coffee to her.

'When you have ordered this', she asked.

Just 10 minutes back, what happened, don't you need it?

No, just asking. You please carry on, she said.

We both were serious. The aura had become silent, she wanted me to tell her more. There were just two more couples sitting at one corner.

So, 20 November 2046. I was in college during my BSC, when I heard 'the lab was jammed with suffocated intoxicant gases and exhaust was also stopped' which had taken away my dad's life. I was totally broken-down Anivehsa, I had lost everything.

I could see her eyes crying and shedding the tears.

'Are you okay, do you want me to stop it here', I asked.

No, please. She hardly said these words. She started crying after that and my eyes also get wet and were just about to shed their load of pain.

After my mom and dad, my uncle and aunt offered me to live with them. But I was hardly comfortable in their lifestyle or vice versa. They did not care about me so much, I had to shift in my dad's house alone.

I knew cooking from my schooling days so, I liked to prepare my food by myself. After my dad's death I had started following him to be a scientist like him and made a goal to work on his invention. I said to her.

Ayan, I am sorry I had asked you to tell this. If I would know that Dr. Brij was your father, then I would have not asked you.

'It's okay, Anivesha', even I want to thank you for today. I too needed someone's shoulder after my parents to cry upon. So, at least don't be sorry for this.

7:00 P.M., third round of coffee.

'Please Anivesha', I offered her third cold coffee.

No…Ayan its 7 I am already late. I had to go. She excused herself.

You are hiding something, Anivesha. I ordered this third coffee so that I can ask you about your story. I could feel the emotions that your eyes are hiding in themselves. Don't you need to tell your story? I asked.

What…? How could you feel it, she asked?

Well it was different that I didn't know your name after studying in the same class for two years. But I remember whenever I saw you, you were always all alone with yourself. You also don't have any friends in college. You do come alone every day, I can feel it.

Yes, I don't have any friends because I don't like their way of living and nor they like mine, simple. She replied.

Is it so simple that in a manner you had just told, well if so I don't think it to be, I said?

What to say Ayan, it is already so late. She added.

I thought with me, you could also share something about you. Please tell me, I too want to know.

She sipped her coffee down the throat in only one stroke.

My life is also screwed like yours. She started.

Hmm,

Actually, I also don't have my mom and dad. They too died when I was just 5 years old. And my grandfather and grandmother had taken over the responsibilities.

When I grow up to 13 years, daddu have also died due to cancer. There was only dadi's income and her smile that had been the reason for my survival otherwise I would have killed myself.

I stood up to hold her. I came near her sofa, she gave a space to me to sit. I hold her from her shoulders by my both hands. She was totally broken down. I could sense how much pain does she had suffered.

Now no more coffee rounds, no more discussion. She had cleared me.

Okay, take this and wipe away your tears, they really don't suit on you. I said, extending my handkerchief to clean off her face.

She wiped out her tears and pasted a fake smile to feel easiness. I knew how hard that smile was. I had also smiled over having my pain down at my heart and memories..

We both came out of the CCD.

I didn't thought this meeting would be emotional one, she said.

Yeah, but it was and sharing our emotions made us feel easy, also after this we get to know about each other more.

Yes, she said smilingly.

You have a very cute smile. I said.

Really, she smiled, well thank you, my dadi also used to say this to me whenever she mock.

The CCD was not so far from our colonies. So, we both get back to our homes soon by a taxi and reached at 8 in night. I had dropped her first, her grandmother was waiting for her outside. We bid goodbyes, I smiled at her dadi and took her blessing by joining both my hands. I reached my house at 8:15 P.M.

The night was so tensed, as so I had tried my best to take all her burden of pains on me. I was not thinking about the bad memories to which I was used to of remembering every night, but her pain has started to bother me more now. Her happiness has become mine, her every pain had started hurting me too, her loneness has started saying much to me. I had started loving her deeply. This was love for which I had cried that night.

DON'T YOU LOVE ME?

Love will wrap me so easily, I have never thought. My heart will feel easy after feeling love for Anivehsa, I have never thought. My feelings were so high about her, I had never thought. Even I would tell Motu about Anivesha and my relationship, I have never thought.

That meeting had changed everything in me and as same as in Anivesha. She had also started loving me which once she had confirmed when we were texting one night. After that we started sharing a lot of time with each other, spending weekends and our loneness at my house, ordering pizza and ice-creams at least thrice a day.

One day, she put forward her intimate desire of having a beer party till late night. I had to agree up on this, as her eyes were so cute that to decline their request was like a big crime for me. I burned her every desire to make her happy. We ordered 4 bottles of corona beer. We gulped them for hours in the night enjoyed our boozing session. My eyes were locking her cuteness in them.

Anivesha has started loving me very much. She was always very excited for our weekends to be together. She even got so naughty at the college time, that many times she had begged me to kiss her while doing practical during leisure time in the lab.

20, September,

Once when Motu was working with me at my house. We were doing assignment which had to be submitted by the next week. It was Sunday and like every weekend Anivesha was to be in my place or might be she was coming that day. Motu was so lazy and carefree that he didn't feel good to inform or discuss with me to plan such working hours. He never did this, nor he informed yesterday about his abrupt coming. He made ashes of my blossoming Sunday by burning it into high fire. My desires were shattered. My heart was cursing him to put on more weight.

How strong do love became that it made me to feel awkward for my dearest friend Motu. But somehow it can also be explained that how it makes you conscious about every detail of your life and of your beloved too.

If Motu could have told me about this. I would manage Anivesha to not to come. But this day I think was also written in the book of my destiny.

Motu was in the house on Sunday. I knew when Anivehsa will arrive, Motu's bloody mind will frame a lot of questions to fire on me.

Half-an-hour passed in surfing through the books and internet in order to complete the assignment. Motu asked me many times why I was looking at the clock or at the door most of the time.

Bell-Rang,

Finally, my status was about to revealed in front of Motu. I knew first he will show his anger, why I have not told him earlier. But when I will offer him a giant party he would be satisfied.

Soon after of the bell rang. I was sure it would be Anivesha. As it had been 8:30A.M when she told me to arrive. I rushed to open the door and to alert Anivesha about Motu. She was wearing black T-shirt which I recommend her, in which she looks much adorable and sexy.

Hi, she said, smiled and hugged me.

I looked back to check Motu and soon after releasing her.

Look, I was sleeping, and Motu came. He didn't inform me, so go back I will call you later. I said foolishly.

'What is this Ayan, I have told you many times that you should tell him about us. Why you are so frightened'. She said in disappointment with her cute eyes. After looking at her delectable eyes I wanted to kiss her, but she was angry, so I let down my desire at the doorsteps.

How and what the need is to tell him. I asked.

Isn't he our friend? She questioned.

Yes, he is. But what is the problem in setting up the matter between us. Why should we popup to tell him.

Are you serious for our relationship, she asked folding her both hands up to her breast, in her decent-anger-look. She was my girl and her that anger look was also one of the most adorable thing that my heart love in her.

Okay! Let's go and tell him. I said in a flurried way. I raised my right hand horizontally to let her go by that way.

Ok! She slammed the door and started moving inside.

Areey! wait, I said shrugging my right hand down hard.

Actually, I didn't want to tell Motu so soon. Because I knew he will get more excited and will demand a big treat for that.

How are you, Nikansh? She said aloud and Nikansh glared at me.

Fine, he answered in a baffling way. I drew my hand to hold and hide my brow and held it like a confused nerdy boy.

"C'mon sit", Motu offered her to sit, she looked in a flurry at me like she had been expecting me to offer her that.

She also has some doubts about the assignment. I said thinking that this could switch the topic for that day.

'Yes, you came at the…right…ti….', Motu was muted by the line of Anivehsa which was bombarded in a jiffy.

"No, actually I need to say something…'", she said looking at me.

'Okay, you are free, so say'. Motu said excitedly.

"I love Ayan". She said. Motu's jaw fallen to his chest. After hearing this. He looked at me surprisingly.

"Tell him, don't you love me". Anivehsa pushed me to pull out my love proof to show him. She signaled me by winking her eyes.

Motu was still in a shock, he put his pen down, left everything and asked. Tell???

"Yes! I love her". Finally, I did what I didn't want to do. I pasted a fake smile to show her my true love.

"Congrats-buddy-and-be-ready", motu texted me on my cell phone. I knew for what he was warning me to get ready and what does his text meant.

I was happy that everything has gone very silently. I thought I would give Motu his treat separately some other day and soon this happened.

Okay! I had a plan, for which I was very excited form many days. Anivehsa's hidden excitement popped up, I looked at her, my brow furrowed. I tried hard to think at what she was up to now?

"We are going goa", Anivesha shocked us in no time. I was frozen, not because I didn't want to spend some time with them, but because of the practical and exam next month and they were planning to waste the couple of day in going goa.

"What", Motu and I said in unison. And my face turned into a sudden wrinkly shock, while Motu seemed to be as excited as she was.

'We will go by car', her excitement was increasing sec by sec.

"Where is car" I asked.

'Your dad's car, isn't it in the garage'. Motu explode out sarcastically and winked at me.

'You didn't tell me', Anivesha questioned.

'Okay! We are going'. So, Finally I had to put my arms down before them. I said smilingly.

THE GOA TRIP

Goa-road-trip,

22nd September.

They reached my house at 9:00 am accordingly as what we discussed. They were exclusively excited. Anivesha came with a bag in which she had her clothes and a purse in which she had her cosmetics. Motu came along with two bags, one is with wheels carrying his clothes and the other one was small one in which he had packed his bloated tummy's demanding items.

We left the selvice at sharp 10:15 A.M in my dad's XUVI. Motu changed up the selected playlist that was my favorite and which I specially saved in my drive.

He logged it out from there and connected his own to play some old Bollywood songs. "Hits of Arijit" was his favorite. "sooraj dooba hai yaaro, do ghuntt nashe ke maaro…" he played this track first. Soon after, Anivesha too got aroused, feeling the "nasha"in the air. She opened the freezer and passed on the beer cans to us.

"CHEERS", we cheered the moment and started enjoying our way.

It took around 5 hours from Bangalore to reach Goa. We could have reach earlier but as Anivehsa got perfectly tuned with Nikansh humorous attitude. They made me to stop at many places, we had lunch in between and they had demanded me to drive at the speed of 80 only. The weather was perfect, cold breezes welcomed us to feel them. We had also stopped our car at the C turn of the flyover from where a beautiful view of the city that we had left behind could be captured. We shot many selfies, photos, also a group photo whose credit goes to my sweet pocket drone, which once I have purchased from Amazon.

After a long drive, finally we were in goa. We left the load of sight-seeing on Anivesha. She had booked a hotel. She selected the beach where we had to go. She selected the church for us to visit, she selected what else she wanted to do in a better way. Even she had selected the drinks we had to enjoy. She was really insane throughout the trip.

We enjoyed at the beach. Even having a bloated tummy, bulging chest which were quite like the breasts, and volleyball sized head, Motu didn't feel ashamed. He undressed himself in front of us and jumped into the sea waiting to gulp him.

I and Anivesha enjoyed in the sea waves driving our love in the water. I kissed her standing there in between other couples and peoples, I know it was not a new thing there, but it was our first kiss which we have done publicly and also, I knelt down on my knees to propose her to make her feel more special that day.

I lifted her up in my arms as it was demanded by Motu. He wanted to click a photograph in that posture. Later when we saw it, we really thanked him for such a beautiful pic. We spend the night in the hotel and on next day we did sight-seeing.

We visited church of St. Cajetan', Anivesha has told me about it. We had our lunch at café bodega specially suggested by Motu to try its taste. Then we went to Agauda Fort and Mahalaxmi Temple after it.

We came back soon as we didn't have much leisure time. Our exams were going to start from the next month. We left goa's outskirts at 7 P.M and reached selvice at around 11P.M. they both stayed that night at my house.

I remember Anivesha, when she came to me late night and woke me up because she was not feeling sleepy. She locked my lips to bribe me for that nonsense. I liked the way she used to disturb me. Her eyes had always conjured over my will and 'Eh' I had to do accordingly. We spent some time together in the other room. I kissed her, she cuddled me tightly and slept there putting her head buried into my chest. I haven't disturbed her. I loved her, I loved her cuteness, I loved her lips, I loved her the way she was sleeping by putting her head on my chest.

BEST MOMENTS

After the Goa trip, the story keeps taking more turns and twists. I was thinking that it was the result of some beautiful program coded by GOD as she too started loving me insanely. We started planning to go out on every weekend. Wc started sharing one ice-cream between us. The last corner seat at the CCD had always been booked at 5 P.M. that was the time we used to meet 4 or 5 times a week.

She had started telling about her every secret and every wish like pizza was her favorite, she love reading books, she likes to spend hours under the black and delectable sky at night. Like dad she also used to tell that she wanted to go in somewhere else that wouldn't have any image of us neither the good one nor the bad one. Not like our world, our people. She wanted to live, where people understand not only to people but also to the nature.

First, days skipped then weeks then months and almost the year 2048 have passed away. We shared everything. When I had to discuss something with Anivesha or when I keep my glances at her during the lectures. She always had her favorite reaction on her face which I think she has specially designed for me. The story had been turning the pages of my life as like what I thought them to turn. The story was passing very smoothly.

How days had skipped the pages of our life? How life changes suddenly. Finally, like everyone I had also got my story like "Everyone has a story".

THE VALENTINE'S DAY

15 February 2049.

4:00 A.M.,

Almost 4 hours had passed discussing all those days of our life that we had counted successfully and yeah this was the 5th surprise for her. It was so special because it has given us the quality time to understand or clear everything about our past lives, about our past love life. Sleep had taken over our eyes to their brim, and hopefully my all the valentine surprises were finished.

She liked it too and said that how so much time had passed yet we didn't feel tired. I lifted her up to take her back to the downstairs. The day, yes, the day on which finally the chapter of "The Propose" has closed. The feelings were very beautiful. Both my heart and mind had won that day.

In the morning 9:00 A.M, I woke up. She was still sleeping. I looked at her for few minutes as she was. Her cuteness was overloaded. I bent to give a sensuous kiss at the most sensitive part of her neck, suddenly she held my neck by her hands, pulled me close to her lips. I was looking into her eyes. She started smiling. We kissed each other, 'The morning kiss'.

I went to the kitchen gulped a glass of water. I brought her a cold coffee. She was still on the bed covered up in her dreams in the half-sleeping mood. Cuddling over the bedspread.

I had to reveal one more secret to her, but I was thinking what she would think about it. But I had to, so I turned towards the other wall of the room. There was a wooden Almira of a good length.

'Anivesha', just last surprise I called her.

What…? She asked, brushing off her eyes and looked at me surprisingly and came ardently.

I said her to close her eyes first. She got very much excited. She closed them with both of her hands. She was looking very cute in that posture.

'Come close', I whispered in her ears.

She smiled and came four steps forward. I slide away that wooden Almira to the nearby corner.

What was this sound? She asked questioningly.

Wait…, I held her shoulders from her back, and said her to start stepping forward. She was feeling everything by her touch of hands, eyes were still closed.

What is this? She asked.

Open it, it's a door.

What! There is door here? She questioned.

This is the surprise Anivehsa, go ahead.

Okay,

She opened it, also her eyes too. She was shocked to see that giant Almira at the corner and the hidden surprise, a room inside my dad's bed room. She entered steeply, looked around and was puzzled.

Is it a lab? She questioned.

I told you na, that after my mom, dad had started to work out his biggest invention.

"Project- The Universe Recreated". She popped it up before the end of my explanation.

Exactly, I said.

She was totally shocked and wanted to bombard a load of question in a flash.

And now you are working on it, right? Does he left any blue print? She asked searching steeply through the documents that were on the table.

How it can be possible. The universe can't be recreated, it seems like an awe theory that humans can create a whole universe. She said smugly. She was so tensed that she shrugged my hand to answer her ardently.

Yes, he left a blue print and more over he left his incomplete model here and yes! we are working on it. I uncovered the model finally in front of her.

"Ohh Myyy GGGOOOODD", she bloated her mouth by this sound.

This model is completed and only the algorithms are left to be generated. I said.

THE LAB,

The lab was like a simple room. My dad had created it himself. He did not want to disclose this invention to anybody else, nor his company, nor me. I saw dad sliding that almirah once when I came back to home after my schooling from Mumbai. I didn't asked dad about it. Nevertheless, the fact was that I wasn't interested in dad's personal life. He himself was very disturbed after my mom's death. I didn't want to bother him more, after all.

And when I was left all alone after my dad, I opened that lab when I was in the 1ˢᵗ year of masters when I shifted to this house. I have told about this to Motu later. Because I was interest taker in physics and so, I took over my dad's invention to complete it.

There was a big table on which dad's personal computer, various chemicals, apparatus that were required for the experiment were arranged. Also, in the left most side of the lab, there was the model made by dad. In the model he created a space to test the big bang experiment.

He believed that if a Big Bang can create a life. Then why can't we create the big bang again, or the life again. He believed this whole cosmos to be a part of binary program. If we will be able to create such codes to design the life, we can create whatever we want to.

This will not be going to be the first experiment related to the big bang theory. Before it, many scientists from different counties have also tried to test this. In 2032, after the research on big bang theory this has been proved that Big Bang can create the life again. But later the big bang experiment was banned when a team of scientist, who was working on this experiment was decomposed in fire.

But dad was sure, that his experiment may be a successful one. He had calculated everything. I was also shocked after checking the blueprint. I mean how does he made this. Everything got cleared to me and I had also started believing that, yes, this experiment may be successful.

To address Motu about this experiment, there was just the only reason, because I did not know the computer codes to create algorithms without which the whole program and machines were useless. The experiment was at a pause there because of algorithms. So, I need to get the help to complete the project. Motu along with me was the part of this experiment. We were very excited to perform it. The mini-scientist of us has been emanating day by day.

When you like music and suppose if you got a chance to sing for a movie. You will do all the possible hard work and will also improve your skills as well and will be very excited to accomplish that. Similarly, that was our condition. Now the experiment had been naked in front of Anivehsa too. She had also joined us.

Now one more prudent mini scientist had joined the team. She was the topper in her bachelor's degree. We had started working passionately on the blue print. We had put each fine concept to understand that experiment. We had also surfed through the internet to fetch all the little information about 'BING BANG THEORY'. We took all our leisure time and burned it to step up on the ladder to get it completed.

Anivesha has also started working hardly on the project with us. Once she has told me that she was very excited for this experiment as it was my dad's idea and his blue print that made our will so strong to work on it.

THE SHOCK

15 May 2049

Motu rang the bell of my house in the morning it was 7:00 A.M. He was pressing the bell like if someone is firing hundreds of bullets from AK-47. I opened the door in my half-sleep mode.

What happened...? I asked.

Where is Anivehsa. He rushed towards our bedroom. He was with his laptop and was quite in a hurry. He called out my name.

Ayan, come fast.

I steeply rushed to see what he is now up to?

He entered the lab with Anivesha. I too followed them to get in.

What's now? I asked him again.

"I have completed the algorithms". He showed the algorithms in his laptop.

We were at the apex of our excitement, even it was hard to believe that he had completed once again. This time he was more confident than ever he was.

We waited for few hours before to check the algorithms and to test the experiment. We assembled the model checked every single detail steeply. Nikansh has worked last time to recheck his algorithms. We had started the project from the beginning, the model was all set. We were preparing everything in a very perfect manner. We worked hard for 10 continuous hours to arrange everything in a sequence.

It was his algorithms that could change everything. It means if we would be able to create such codes and programs to generate the life, then we can also understand the coding of our life. We could change the negativities from humans to live happily and equally. We could change this nature accordingly. We could control the life and its processes. We could lead this life to some other directions.

Actually, dad worked on nucleic acids and their structures, how they can regenerate. He made a machine for Big Bang. He believed that if the model and the machine on which that model depends on, will become invisible then the project will be successful. That means 'That Recreated Universe' will get lost in the cosmos, and a new universe will be created and will hold its position somewhere in the cosmos'.

We all knew that the experiment would be risky, and we could have to pay something bigger than what we had not even thought of. But we were very excited about the experiment, as we had given a lot of time to it. To test the experiment, we had trapped a rat. After all, it was all about to make a tissue invisible, so we had to take 'our brave rat' in the experiment. If the rat got invisible, we will be successful.

What are you writing 'Ayan'? Anivesha asked me. When almost only half-an-hour was left, and everything was ready.

Nothing just a story what we are doing, I said them insanely.

They didn't, even not Anivesha knew, 'I was writing our story from the beginning '.

Nikansh had loaded the algorithms and finally the program was completely ready. We had done all these arrangements, many times to match the algorithms and this was not our first try to test this experiment.

Which try is it, Anivesha? I asked.

6th, she said

Anivehsa pointed towards me by the screw driver with which she was working on the machine.

This would be going to be our 7th try and I crossed my fingers to wish it to work this time.

Could you please put your diary down, Nikansh shouted?

I was very excited, I just laughed at him, 'THE MOTU'.

I excused myself, wait a minute I am coming.

Now, where are you going? They both screamed together.

I just laughed at both of them and came out to finish this story and to put it in the bookshelf.

The last paragraph,

If this experiment succeeds, I will complete this story and will try to publish it in golden letter. "THE UNIVERSE RECREATED".

And if something happened wrong to this experiment. Then only you, my diary you at least you will remember me as your author.

Goodbye,

Take care,

See you soon,

I love you.

-AYAN

17 May 2049

When I turned the last page of the calendar diary, many questions steeply raised in my mind. But the diary had only those pages describing only the story of Ayan and Anivesha.

It took full one day time period to read out this diary "2048". I flipped my fingers over the pages of the diary for more pages to reveal the truth. Where all they had gone? Did they die? Or like mentioned in the diary that "if the experiment would be successful then the rat will get lost into the new universe they created into the cosmos". Are they lost there in the time? All these questions were churning my mind insanely. The flipping pages of that "Calendar diary" had turned me as an insane reader.

After reading this diary, on the same day I went to the Collins street again to visit Ayan's house, to see that lab again. I was thinking where did they have gone or lost?

Their love made me cry. Ayan and Anivesha had got their love at so last in their pages of life. I was totally broken to see the lab again. My eyes started crying. I prayed to GOD to take care of them where they have gone or lost. I scratched my back against the wall down to the floor and cried hard. How this could be written in the story of his destiny. How could GOD program such lives for someone.

Well in the eyes of world the case will show that the leaked news of this experiment was a rumor, but what to tell myself? I found myself sinking into the vast and deep ocean of many questions about "THE PROJECT UNIVERSE RECREATED".

Are they lost?

Are they dead?

What would have happened to them?

To be continued...